Contents

Chapter 1

What has Happened to Mad Iris?

Not every school has an ostrich. That's what made Pudding Lane School so special. They *did* have an ostrich. It wasn't a pretend one, or a toy one, or a stuffed one. It was a real ostrich. Her name was Mad Iris.

Mad Iris had run away from an ostrich farm. She ran all the way to Pudding Lane School. The teachers tried to chase Mad Iris away, but the children liked her. She ate their pencils and then they had to stop doing their work. Mad Iris liked the children too, because she liked to eat pencils. The children wanted her to stay.

Then the men from the ostrich farm came to get Mad Iris. Ross and his friend Katie hid her in the boys' toilets. Katie *says* she's Ross's girl-friend, but Ross says they're just ordinary friends.

The men chased Ross and Mad Iris onto the flat roof of the school. They wanted to shoot Mad Iris, but Mr Grimble, the headteacher, stopped them. That was when the school said that Mad Iris could stay. She became their mascot.

Katie wasn't on the roof with Ross and Mad Iris. She had got her feet stuck in a toilet bowl. It took a long time to get her out. If you want to know more about that you can read *Mad Iris*, which is the first book about Mad Iris.

Mad Iris moved into the caretaker's shed. The caretaker didn't like that, so he had to find somewhere else to go. He shared the cook's little office with her. He liked that, and the cook liked that and soon they got married. But that's another story.

Mad Iris liked the caretaker's shed because it was full of funny things that made funny noises when she ate them. They often had funny tastes too. For example, she once ate a bit of rubber tube. It made squeaky noises in her beak and it tasted of ... well, it tasted of rubber.

Another time, Mad Iris ate a small pack of screws. Mad Iris wasn't sure if she liked screws. They were a bit hard to chew, but she liked the silver colour. She tried to eat the screw-driver too, but she was sure she did

not like the screw-driver. It was too sharp. She spat it out. Then she stamped on it and kicked it under a cupboard.

Everyone at Pudding Lane liked having an ostrich as their school mascot. No other school had a mascot like Mad Iris. Bottom End School had a fluffy pink teddy. Top End School *said* they had a real shark but nobody at Pudding Lane believed that. Well, only the Year Ones. But then most of the Year Ones also believed Mr Grimble had super powers. He didn't.

So the children at Pudding Lane School were very happy, and so was Mad Iris.

But then, one morning, Ross and Katie and their friends went to say "Hello" to Mad Iris, like they did every morning. They opened the shed door. Mad Iris wasn't there!

MAD IRIS HAD GONE!

Chapter 2
Ross Thinks Hard

"Where is she?" Katie asked.

"I don't know," Ross snapped. Then he spotted a scrap of paper on the floor and picked it up. "It's a note," he said.

"What does it say?" asked Ross's friend Buster.

"It says HA HA," Ross said.

"Ha ha?" Katie asked. "What's that supposed to mean?"

Ross glared at her. "How am I supposed to know? That's all it says."

"Someone is playing a trick on us," Katie said.

Buster nodded. "Do you think the teachers are having a joke?" he asked.

They went to see Mrs Norton, their teacher. They told her that Mad Iris had gone. Mrs Norton was very surprised and she said she didn't know anything about it. Then they all went to see the Head Teacher, Mr Grimble.

Mr Grimble rushed to the shed and peered in. "Oh dear," he said. "She must have got out!"

"She left a note," Buster said.

"Don't be silly!" said Ross. "Mad Iris can't write! Somebody else left the note, and that means somebody else was here."

Ross showed Mr Grimble the note. "Do you know what?" said Mr Grimble. "I think Mad Iris has been kidnapped."

"Kidnapped?" gasped Ross and Katie. "Why would anyone want to kidnap an ostrich?"

"I don't know," said Mr Grimble. "But this has happened at a very bad time. We've got the football final against Top End School at the end of the week. They always beat us in the final and win the cup."

"That's because they cheat," said Katie, with a frown. Katie was one of the stars of the football team.

"Maybe they do," Mr Grimble said. "Even so, I did hope we would beat them this year. It would be fantastic if we could beat Top End at last. I thought Mad Iris would bring us good luck!"

Ross was staring at the ground. He frowned a bit. Then he frowned a bit more and then he frowned a lot.

"What's up with you?" Buster asked.

"I'm thinking," Ross said. "Isn't it odd that Mad Iris has been kidnapped just when we need her most?" Then he smiled. "Who would want to do that?" he asked.

"Who?" asked Mrs Norton. "We don't know. Do you?"

"I think I have an idea," Ross said.

"Tell us then!" shouted the others.

Ross smiled again. "Top End School! It's just the sort of nasty trick they would pull.

They've stolen Mad Iris to make sure we don't win on Friday."

Mr Grimble looked at Mrs Norton. "He could be right," he said.

Mrs Norton looked at Buster. "He could be right," she said.

Buster looked at Katie. "He could be right," he said.

Katie beamed a big smile at Ross. "You are so clever. I always knew you were brainy as well as good looking."

"Oooh!" said Mrs Norton, with a wink. "Who's a lucky boy?"

Ross stopped smiling. His face turned very, very red. But secretly he was very, very pleased!

Mr Grimble stamped back to his office. "I am going to speak to the Head Teacher at Top End School. I am going to ring her right now and ask for our ostrich back."

Chapter 3
Trouble at Top End Primary

The Head Teacher of Top End School was called Miss Sly. When Mr Grimble rang Miss Sly was having a bad time. This was because Mad Iris was in her office.

Mad Iris liked phones. She liked to pick them up and bang them on hard things like tables and Miss Sly's head. Miss Sly's head made lots of noises when Mad Iris hit it with the phone. It went "OW!" and "STOPPITT!"

All this made life very hard for Miss Sly. It was hard to have a proper talk with Mr Grimble. "Why on earth would we want to steal your ostrich, Mr Grimble?" she snapped.

"Because you want to stop us winning the cup on Friday," Mr Grimble said.

"Don't be so silly," Miss Sly said to Mr Grimble. "*Ow! Gerroff!*" she said to Mad Iris as Mad Iris pecked her hand.

Then Mad Iris grabbed the phone in her beak and shook it to see if it rattled. It didn't. How boring. So Mad Iris stuffed the phone inside Miss Sly's shirt.

"Wargh! Argh!" screamed Miss Sly. The school secretary rushed into Miss Sly's office. She screamed too. The school secretary wasn't being attacked or anything. She just *liked* screaming.

"Aargh!"

Mad Iris thought all the noise was great. She was having so much fun that she even chased Miss Sly and the secretary up and down the corridor for a bit.

At the other end of the line Mr Grimble smiled. Only one thing could cause so much havoc – Mad Iris. Now he knew that Top End School had kidnapped her.

But how on earth could Pudding Lane get Mad Iris back?

"We should go over there and get her," said Mrs Norton.

Mr Grimble shook his head. "We can't just walk in and ask for our ostrich back. Top End will call the police. And I bet they'll hide Mad Iris somewhere until the match is over."

The two teachers looked at each other and gave a sigh. They had no idea what to do.

Chapter 4
Who is Monstermash?

Mr Grimble and Mrs Norton had no plan for how to get Mad Iris back. So that left everything up to Ross and his class. They talked about it for the whole of break. Ian Tufnell had the first idea. He was a big boy and good at judo.

"Let's burst in and grab her," he said. There was a war-like glint in his eyes.

"The teachers will stop us," Katie said.

"We'll tie them to their chairs!"

Katie shook her head. "Ian, there are more of them than there are of us. If anyone gets tied to chairs, it will be us!"

"She's right," said Buster with a nod.

"No way," said Ian. "I can do judo."

"Yeah? Well I can do origami," said Ross, and he winked at Katie.

"Origami is folding paper!" Katie said. "How's that going to help?"

"It'll give them a surprise," said Ross with a laugh. "And while they watch me do origami, you can save Mad Iris."

Ian Tufnell glared at Katie and Ross. "You're stupid," he said.

"So is trying to beat up a lot of teachers with judo," said Ross.

"So what's your plan then, clever clogs?" asked Ian.

Ross and Katie looked at each other. No, they didn't have a plan.

"Idiots," said Ian, and he stomped off.

Katie waited until Ian was gone. Then she told Ross and Buster that she *did* have a plan. "We'll break into the school in the middle of the night and save Iris," she said.

Buster didn't think this idea would work. "The school will have an alarm," he said. "We'll set it off."

"Maybe we could get in and out before the police arrive," said Ross. But Buster shook his head again. It was a big risk.

Then Katie grabbed their arms. Her eyes were shiny. "How about we just walk in? We can go in the morning like everyone else. If we wear the Top End uniform no one will notice us."

"Where are we going to get Top End uniforms from?" asked Ross.

Katie was almost jumping up and down with excitement. "That boy next door to you! He goes to Top End. His mum washes his uniform and hangs it up in the back garden to dry. All you have to do is nip over the fence and nick it!"

Ross stared in horror. He could see why Katie thought the plan would work. The boy next door did go to Top End. But Ross could also see a problem.

"That boy is called Monstermash," Ross said.

"Why?" asked Buster.

"Because he's a monster and he mashes people," Ross told him. "So I have to steal a school uniform from a monster masher, get into Top End, find Mad Iris and save her. I'm so dead." Ross sat down with a sigh.

"Don't worry," Katie she said. "I'll kiss it better for you."

"Oh double great," said Ross, with an even bigger sigh.

Chapter 5
Watch Out for Custard Man!

Up at Top End, no one was making any fun for Mad Iris. Mad Iris decided that she would just have to make some fun for Top End.

The first thing she did was to take assembly. As you may know, ostriches are not supposed to take assembly. But Mad Iris was not a normal ostrich. She waited until Miss Sly had stood up in front of all the children. Then Mad Iris took over.

"Please stand," said Miss Sly to the children. "We will now sing *Morning has …* waaaaargh!" Mad Iris's head suddenly popped up behind Miss Sly. Mad Iris grabbed Miss Sly's song book and threw it at the front row.

"I'll save you, Miss Sly!" yelled Mr Dubbin, the Deputy Head. He flung himself at Mad Iris and somehow he landed on her back. Mad Iris took off at once, with Mr Dubbin clinging to her neck.

Off Mad Iris went, away down the corridor. SPLIP! SPLAP! went her great big feet as she raced along.

"Help!" yelled Mr Dubbin. "I'm being kidnapped by an ostrich!"

Mad Iris dashed into the school kitchen. The cooks began to scream and dropped all their pots and pans. Mad Iris didn't like all the noise. She stuffed her head into a giant

bowl of cold custard so that she couldn't hear
it any more.

When Mad Iris put her head in the
custard, Mr Dubbin slid down her long, thin
neck, hit the side of the custard bowl and
then fell on the floor. The bowl wobbled and
all the custard tipped onto Mr Dubbin's head.

"You idiots!" yelled the cooks. "There will
be no pudding now! Get out!" They picked up
their egg whisks and big wooden spoons and
chased Mr Dubbin and Mad Iris back out into
the corridor.

Mad Iris went SPLIP SPLAP SLIP SPLAP
back down the corridor, shaking her head to
get the custard off. Behind her was Mr
Dubbin. And behind him were three very
cross cooks.

Back in the hall Miss Sly was trying to
calm the children down. But when Mad Iris
and Mr Dubbin and the cooks ran in the

children all began to scream again. A sloppy yellow monster was on the loose! And a mad ostrich! Teachers and children ran in all directions. Some climbed up the wallbars in the hall. Some hid behind chairs.

Poor Mr Dubbin was nearly blind because his eyes were full of custard. (So were his ears and nose and just about every other part of him.) He kept bumping into people.

Mad Iris still wanted to get away from all the noise. At last she found a small room with nobody in it. It was the library. Iris peered at all the books. They looked very nice. Would they taste nice too? She ate one, and it did. So she ate another.

In the corridor outside, Miss Sly was creeping up to the library door. BANG!! She slammed it shut. Mad Iris was a prisoner. Miss Sly gave a big sigh of relief. At last everyone was safe.

Just then there was a terrible noise from the far end of the corridor and a sloppy yellow madman came charging along! Behind the madman were three cooks, who were hurling plates and spoons and forks at him.

"STOP THIS AT ONCE!" Miss Sly roared. Then she was hit by a flying saucer. A real flying saucer! She fell in a heap on the floor.

So that was the end of assembly at Top End School.

Chapter 6
Ross Gets Brave

In an odd way Mad Iris and her assembly helped Ross a lot. Half the children from Top End School went home splattered with custard. Monstermash was one of them. His mum made him take off his uniform at once. It went straight into the washing machine. An hour later it was hanging out to dry on the line in the garden.

Ross waited until it was getting dark. He knew that Monstermash's mum would take the uniform back down very soon. He had to get into Monstermash's garden and grab it.

"OK," he said to himself. "I have got to do this. I shall count to three. One, two, three ..." But it was no good. Ross was too scared to do it.

"I must be brave," he told himself. "This time I won't chicken out. OK. Here we go. one, two, er, two and half, er, two and three quarters, er … THREE! GO! GO! GO!"

Ross jumped over the fence into Monstermash's garden. He raced across the grass. He grabbed the sweatshirt and snatched the trousers and dashed back. He was back over the fence again in one jump.

"I am the champion!" he yelled. Then he had to hide behind the shed as Monstermash's mum came out to take in the washing. She stopped. She scratched her head. She looked all around. Something was missing. She shook her head a few times and went back inside.

Ross grinned. He stuffed the uniform up his jumper and sneaked back inside. His heart was thumping like all the drums in a drum kit, but he felt fantastic. He'd done it!

All he had to do now was walk into Top End School the next morning.

Aaaaaaaaaaaaaarrrgh!!!

Ross turned white from top to toe. *What was he thinking? How could he get away with it? Was he mad? Was he crazy? Would he get killed a hundred times over?* Probably.

GULP!

Chapter 7
Ross Gets Even Braver

The next morning was Friday morning. It was the day of the football final. Ross and Katie stood outside Top End School and watched the children going in.

"They look very big," said Ross.

"You'll be fine," said Katie.

"I look like an idiot in this uniform," Ross moaned.

It was true. Ross *did* look like an idiot. Monstermash was very big. Some people might even say that he was *too* big. They just wouldn't say it when he was listening. Monstermash's trousers were too long for Ross and much too baggy round the middle. The sweatshirt was too big and the sleeves dangled a long way past Ross's hands.

"I'm going to get killed," said Ross.

"No you're not," said Katie. "You're going to go into the school. You're going to find Mad Iris and you're going to rescue her. Then you'll be a big hero and you'll get to marry the princess, just like a fairy tale."

"I suppose you're the princess?" Ross asked with a scowl. Katie beamed up at him and nodded. Ross shook his head. "I'd better get going," he said.

"Good luck," said Katie, and blew him a kiss.

Ross turned very red and rushed towards the school. At any moment he thought someone would grab him and say: "Hey! You're not from this school!" But he got through the front gate and nobody said a word. He got through the front door and still nobody stopped him. After that Ross began to think that he might just be able to do this amazing thing. He might find Iris. He might save her. He might become a hero – a real hero! He might marry the princess!

Noooooo! Nightmare!! He didn't want to marry any princesses!!!

"Hey!" said a voice. "You boy!" Ross stopped and swung round. He found himself face-to-face with Miss Sly, the Head Teacher. She had a plaster above her eye where she'd been hit by a flying saucer the day before. It made her look a bit like a pirate. She was scary!

"Where are you going?" Miss Sly asked. "You know the classrooms are back that way. Whose class are you in?"

Ross was in a panic. He didn't know the name of any teachers at Top End. As he tried to think of something to say, Miss Sly peered at him.

"Are those your trousers?" she asked. "They look rather big."

"They're my brother's," Ross said. "I wet mine." He gritted his teeth. How could he have said such a stupid thing?

"You WET your trousers?" Miss Sly asked.

"I mean I spilled my drink on them," Ross said, as fast as he could. "This morning. At breakfast. Milk."

Miss Sly shook her head. "You're a funny boy. Well, don't just stand there like a fool. Get to your class."

Phew! That was a narrow escape! Ross turned and rushed back down the corridor. As he walked he looked into the rooms on both sides. And there she was! Mad Iris! She was in the ... well, what room was it? Ross thought it might have been the library once. Now it looked a bit ... odd.

Mad Iris had picked up every single book. She'd pecked them and kicked them. She'd thrown them at the windows. She'd thrown them at the walls and ceiling. She'd played football with them. In fact, Mad Iris had done just about everything she could do to them, except read them.

Ross checked that nobody was looking and slipped into the room. Mad Iris was so pleased to see Ross. She liked him. He was fun. She went straight across to him and tried to pull all his hair out.

"Stop it!" hissed Ross. "Don't worry. I've come to save you. We're going to escape."

Mad Iris picked up what was left of a book about Vikings and tried to stuff it down the back of Ross's sweatshirt. He grabbed it from her. "Stop it!" he said. "Behave yourself."

Ross's heart was beating like a drum kit again. He and Mad Iris had to make their escape *now*.

"Follow me," he whispered to Mad Iris. "Don't make a sound."

Chapter 8
Ross Gets a Reward

"Come on," said Ross. "And shhh!"

Mad Iris and Ross stepped into the corridor. BANG!

What on earth had made that noise? It was Mad Iris. She was stuck in the door. She had a chair in her beak and she was trying to take it out of the library with her. Ross pushed her back into the room as fast as he could and took the chair away. "I told you to behave," he said in a cross voice. "Now let's try again."

This time they got out the door without any problems. At the end of the corridor was the front door and after that – freedom. Ross kept his eyes on the front door and marched towards it. Just then a classroom door opened and out came a boy. It was Monstermash!

Monstermash stood right in front of Ross and stared at him. Did he know who Ross was? After all, Ross lived next door to him.

"Don't I ...?" began Monstermash.

"No you don't," said Ross, and shook his head. But Monstermash just stared and stared at him. He was right in front of Ross, so Ross couldn't move.

"Aren't you ...?" Monstermash began again.

"No I'm not," said Ross, with a bigger shake of his head.

Monstermash peered at Ross's clothes. "Aren't those ...?" he began.

"No they aren't," said Ross. "Well, I must get going. Got to take the ostrich to the vet. She needs to get her toenails clipped."

Monstermash looked down at Iris's feet. She did have very long toenails. He moved to one side. Ross pulled Iris after him and rushed down the corridor. A few seconds later he was pushing the front door open and then they were outside. Freedom!

Ross tried not to run down the school path but when Mad Iris saw Katie she began to gallop towards her. Katie threw her arms round the ostrich's neck.

"Oh Iris," she said. "It's so good to see you." Mad Iris was pleased to see Katie too so she ate Katie's tie. Well, she tried, but it was still tied to Katie's neck, which made things tricky for both of them.

"I did it!" said Ross. "I did it!"

"My hero!" smiled Katie, and kissed Ross on the cheek.

"Yuck!" went Ross. After all the danger he'd been in he'd been got in the end!

Chapter 9
The Cup Final

The cup final was held at Pudding Lane. Mr Grimble had kept Mad Iris hidden until the match began. "She'll be a surprise," he said.

Katie and the Pudding Lane team were shocked when they saw how big the Top End players were. They looked enormous and they stood in a row and grinned like tigers at the Pudding Lane team.

"We're going to get killed," said Buster. "What kind of flowers would you like on your grave, Katie?"

"Poppies," said Katie, and the match began.

In fact, Top End were not very good at football. But they were very good at fouls when the ref wasn't looking. They tried every trick in the book. Before long Top End had scored three goals and Pudding Lane were 3 – 0 down.

That was the moment that Mr Grimble decided to bring out Mad Iris. He took her all round the pitch. A great cheer went up from Pudding Lane and Mad Iris marched up and down, her eye on the ball. That football was the most fun thing Mad Iris had seen for ages. She did a little dance, pounding the ground with her feet, as if she were getting ready for a penalty kick.

As soon as they saw Mad Iris, the Pudding Lane players got a new burst of life. Moments later Katie and Buster both scored goals. The score was 3 – 2. Top End were raging. Monstermash kicked Buster so hard that Buster was put out of the game. He had to be taken off on a stretcher.

Once again Top End was in control of the game and they scored again. But Katie didn't give up and minutes later she scored Pudding Lane's 3rd goal.

Monstermash was raging. "Girls shouldn't play football," he hissed, and he stamped on Katie's foot. Hard.

"Argh!" Katie crashed to the ground. She hugged her hurt leg.

"You can't do that!" Ross yelled. But the ref hadn't seen it happen.

"Oh, I am SO sorry," said Monstermash with a nasty smile. "Did I hurt the little girlie?"

Ross helped Katie limp to the side. She was out of the game now so Pudding Lane were down to nine players. After that it was easy for Top End. They scored again and again. It was so hard to watch that some Pudding Lane pupils started to drift off home. Ross was so angry he didn't know what to do.

But Mad Iris did. She marched onto the pitch and went straight for that wonderful black and white ball. She kicked it. She pushed it with her beak. She raced up the pitch and BANG!

"Goal!" yelled Ross.

"She can't play!" yelled the Top End players. "She's an ostrich! Hey, ref – get that ostrich sent off."

But the ref said there was nothing in the rules to say that ostriches couldn't play football. Ross said that Iris was a substitute for the two hurt players. The ref was quite happy with that and so the game went on.

It wasn't long before the score was 10 all. There was only one minute of play left. Someone kicked the ball way up into the air. Up and up it went. Everyone rushed over to it, but Mad Iris was ahead of them. She pushed past them all and with one great jump she soared up into the air and BAM! she headed the ball so hard it almost took the goalie's head off. The ball shot straight into the back of the net.

The ref blew his whistle and that was it – Pudding Lane had won! 11 – 10!

The school had never been so happy. Everyone cheered, even the caretaker and the cook.

Miss Sly had to hand over the cup to Mr Grimble. Mr Grimble was just a bit too slow, so Mad Iris grabbed it and went racing round and round the school with it. She had decided that the cup was hers, and she was right really. After all, she'd scored the winning goal.

"How's your foot?" Ross asked Katie.

"It's a bit sore," she answered. She had an ice pack on it. She gave Ross a big smile and lifted off the ice pack. "It just needs to be kissed better," she said.

Ross turned white. He would do almost anything for Katie. He had nicked a school uniform from right under Monstermash's nose. He had got into Top End Primary and saved Mad Iris. He had faced almost certain death! But there had to be limits. NO WAY was he going to KISS KATIE'S FOOT!